*To Grumpy Tammy!*
*~With Love, Julia*

W9-CTX-820

# Baditude!

## (What to do when your life STINKS!)

Boys Town, Nebraska

Written by **Julia Cook**

Illustrated by **Anita DuFalla**

**Baditude! What to Do When Your Life Stinks!**
Text and Illustrations Copyright © 2015 by Father Flanagan's Boys' Home
ISBN 978-1-934490-90-7

Published by the Boys Town Press
14100 Crawford St.
Boys Town, NE 68010

All rights reserved under International and Pan-American Copyright Conventions. Unless otherwise noted, no part of this book may be reproduced, stored in a retrieval system, or transmitted in any form or by any means, electronic, mechanical, photocopying, recording or otherwise, without express written permission of the publisher, except for brief quotations or critical reviews.

For a Boys Town Press catalog, call **1-800-282-6657**
or visit our website: **BoysTownPress.org**

Publisher's Cataloging-in-Publication Data

Cook, Julia, 1964-

Baditude! : what to do when your life stinks! / written by Julia Cook ; illustrated by Anita DuFalla.
-- Boys Town, NE : Boys Town Press, [2015]

pages ; cm.
(Responsible me!)

ISBN: 978-1-934490-90-7
Audience: grades K-6.
Summary: Noodle's attitude is alienating everyone around him. Can he let go of his angst and try to find the brighter side of life? With help from a teacher and his mom, Noodle learns how to turn his 'have to's' into 'get to's' and his baditude into gratitude!--Publisher.

1. Children--Life skills guides--Juvenile fiction. 2. Attitude change in children--Juvenile fiction. 3. Change (Psychology)--Juvenile fiction. 4. Anger in children--Juvenile fiction. 5. Temper tantrums in children-- Juvenile fiction. 6. Child psychology. 7. Problem children--Behavior modification. 8. [Conduct of life--Fiction. 9. Attitude (Psychology)-- Fiction. 10. Change (Psychology)--Fiction. 11. Anger--Fiction. 12. Temper tantrums--Fiction. 13. Behavior.] I. DuFalla, Anita. II. Title. III. Series.

PZ7.C76984 B33    2015
E        1508

*Printed in the United States*
10  9  8  7  6  5  4  3

Boys Town Press is the publishing division of Boys Town, a national organization serving children and families.

My name is Norman David Edwards...
but everybody calls me
"Noodle."

Some days,
**my life just**
STINKS!!!

3

I love to sleep in, but every morning my mom makes me get up about **100 HOURS TOO EARLY.** School starts at 8:00 and it only takes me 10 minutes to get there, so I could sleep in until 7:45 and be just fine,

# but NO!

I have to set my alarm for 6:50!!! **Getting up early** STINKS!

**NO VIDEO GAMES ON SCHOOL PREMISES**

Then, when I get to school, I can't play any video games at ALL!

That just STINKS!

Please write your answers in complete sentences.

If I don't get my homework done, my teacher makes me stay in from morning recess and do it.

That STINKS!

Last night, I did all of my homework and I still had to stay in!

"Noodle... On this assignment, your answers need to be written in complete sentences."

Complete sentences STINK!

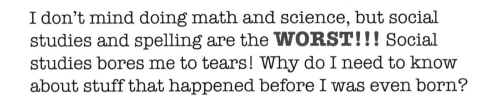

I don't mind doing math and science, but social studies and spelling are the **WORST!!!** Social studies bores me to tears! Why do I need to know about stuff that happened before I was even born?

And spelling? Why do I need to know how to spell every word correctly? Isn't that what spell check is for?

Then, there's Language Arts... I actually think they gave it that name to make it sound more fun... It didn't work!

Then, every single Friday, we have to take a spelling test along with a gazillion other tests. I seriously think that my teacher's name is "Mrs. – Give Me Another Test – Jones!"

Tests STINK!

X serenipidy
X gargancuon
ridiculous
epidemy
X complycation
bullyan
clairvoiant

Four score and seven years

Language ARTS

**TODAY'S SCHEDULE**
9:30 PhysEd
10:30 Social Studies unit seven test
12:05 Reading Test chapters 8-11
1:00 Math chapter 6 test
2:00 practice for Science Fair

And *to top it all off...*
My teacher made me move my
desk next to **Mary Gold!!!**

**Girls**
# STINK!

Some days after school, my life gets even worse!

On Mondays and Wednesdays, I have to go to soccer practice. I love to play in the games, but practice STINKS! Our coach makes us do dumb drills over and over again and then we have to run about a

# gazillion miles!

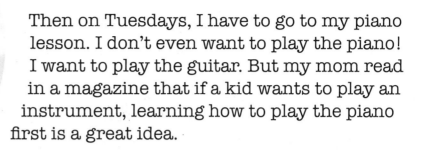

Then on Tuesdays, I have to go to my piano lesson. I don't even want to play the piano! I want to play the guitar. But my mom read in a magazine that if a kid wants to play an instrument, learning how to play the piano first is a great idea.

The worst part of all about piano lessons is that my teacher, Mr. Panini, has the STINKIEST breath on the planet!

9

Thursdays and Fridays aren't too bad. They're my **free days!** After school, I get to do anything I want to.

Today, I went to Dominic's house to play... But he had too much homework.

**Homework** STINKS!

So then, I went to Reginald's... But he had to mow the lawn.

**Yard work** STINKS!

I went to John's, but he wasn't home.

Jake said he had the flu.

And Curtis had to get all dressed up for family pictures!

**Family pictures REALLY STINK!**

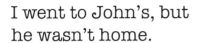

I decided to go home and just play video games. But my battery was dead and my mom had my charging cord in her purse.

**Dead batteries STINK!**

I turned on the TV to watch SLIME MAN.

**A rerun!!!! Reruns STINK!!!**

Just then, my mom came home from work.

"How was your day, Noodle?" she asked me.

"IT STUNK!" I said.

"Why?"

"I got a detention for getting to school late.
I had to miss morning recess because I made a few mistakes.

Math and science went OK, but spelling was the worst.
Social studies is boring, and my desk got moved by girls!

My teacher gave us homework
and it's Thursday... MY FREE DAY!
I went to all of my friends' houses,
and none of them could play.

I came home to play my video games,
but you still have my cord.
Slime Man was a rerun and now

I'm
SUPER
BORED!"

**"Cheer up, Noodle.** Tonight we're having lasagna for dinner...**your favorite!"**

**"That** STINKS!
I have dishes tonight and it takes me a gazillion years to get the lasagna pan clean!!!"

**"Cheer up, Noodle.** I'm sure some of your friends can play tomorrow after school."

"That's a whole day from now!"

14

"**Cheer up, Noodle.** Tomorrow is your school science fair, and you have such a great project this year!"

"I probably won't win...
Science Fairs STINK!"

15

"Noodle, does anything
in your life smell good?"

"You tell me that everything stinks.
But I want you to stop and think.

There is good everywhere
if you know where to look.
Even in the kitchen sink!"

"Huh?"

"It sounds to me like you have a

# 'Baditude.'"

"A 'Baditude'... What's that?"

*"'Baditude' is short for a 'bad attitude.'
Your face has a unibrow and
 you're in a bad mood.*

*Nothing sounds good in your life today.
You have a 'Baditude' and
 it's getting in your way!!!"*

"Noodle, you get to choose how you see the world that you live in.

# The more you complain about things, the more things you will find to complain about!

Your 'Baditude' is causing you to have a pity party, and you're trying to invite everyone around you. I don't think anybody's going to show up!"

"What?"

"Noodle, in order to have a good life, you need to have a positive view of your future. You need to figure out how to change your

BADITUDE.

into

Gratitude

and become more thankful for the world that you are a part of."

"Yeah, but how do I do that?"

"It's not hard, Noodle, to figure it out,
you just need to do three things.
Look for the positives in all situations.
Life's not as bad as it seems.

Then turn your orders into opportunities.
Turn your **'HAVE TO'S'** into **'GET TO'S'**.
And always remember, attitude is contagious.
It spreads just like colds and the flu."

{recipe}

BADITUDE

to

*Gratitude*

**1** Look for the positives.

**2** Turn your 'Have To's' into 'Get To's'.

**3** If you wear a unibrow on your face, others will do the same.

"If you wear a unibrow on your face,
    others will do the same.
But if you choose to smile instead of frown,
    you're sure to win at life's game!"

"What are you talking about, Mom?"

"Well, getting up early during the week makes sleeping in on the weekends that much more special. And, your teacher wants you to be on time for school because

## school is practice for life.

Someday when you have a real job, you won't be able to keep it if you don't show up on time."

"Learning more about social studies, spelling and language arts is only going to make learning about math and science easier and more fun!

And my lasagna is going to make your mouth SO happy that your hands won't even mind cleaning up the pan!"

"You **'GET TO'** learn how to play the piano so that when you do take guitar lessons, you'll be really good at it!

You **'GET TO'** go to soccer practices. You 'GET TO' see your teammates during the week. You'll 'GET' great exercise, which will help you stay healthy. And you 'GET TO' learn and develop your skills so that you can become a better player!

You **'GET TO'** be a part of the Science Fair, and it's going to be so much fun!!!"

"Noodle, life is like looking into a thousand mirrors. If you give yourself a unibrow... 1000 unibrows will be staring back at you, and **YOUR LIFE WILL STINK!**

But if you SMILE, you'll be amazed at how many people will smile back, and your life will start smelling a whole lot better!"

24

I went into the bathroom and looked into the mirror. My mom was right!!

# I did have a unibrow.

I decided to take her advice and work on switching my

BADITUDE

*to*

*Gratitude*

That night, my mom helped me do the dishes, and the lasagna pan wasn't even that bad because **my mouth was so happy!!!** (That was the best lasagna EVER!)

I went to bed early so that getting up at 6:50 wasn't quite as terrible.

**I smiled when I aced my spelling test.** (Studying every day this week really paid off!)

I used my new soccer move at recess and made a goal and that made me feel good inside. (Maybe soccer practice isn't so bad after all!)

We actually did ART in language arts today!

Social studies didn't seem as bad either. I worked with Reginald. We got all of our questions answered, and we even had time to spare. We even wrote them out in complete sentences. Then Reginald invited me over to his house to play after school!

# Science Fair Today

I didn't win the Science Fair,
but I did get a 3rd place medal!
(Maybe next year.)

Today my life didn't seem quite as bad.
I had a lot of fun, and I didn't get mad.
I smiled at others and
they smiled back.
My attitude's better and
I'm getting on track.

Watering a Plant
with Other Liquids

Milk

Orange
juice

Water

3rd

My mom was right, I had a 'Baditude.'
It made me frown and even act rude!
What my mom said to me really made me think.
**I realize now that my life doesn't STINK!**

But I still can't play video games at school,

AND I have to sit next to a GIRL!

And that really really really really really really

# STINKS!!!

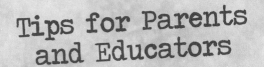

# Turning BADITUDE into *Gratitude*

Attitude is a small word that impacts life in a huge way. Many experts believe attitude is more important than education, money, circumstances, failures, successes, giftedness, skills, and appearance. There are things you can control and things you cannot. For example, a person cannot control events that have happened in the past, the inevitable, or the way another person chooses to act. A person can, however, control his/her attitude about those things.

### Teaching a child to change a negative attitude into a positive one can be a difficult process. Here are a few tips that might help.

**1.** Help children develop a better understanding of how negativity affects them. You can control how you feel!

**2.** Teach children that whenever they see a negative they should actively look for a positive to cancel out the negative. Train children to actively look for the positives in all situations (i.e., Oversleeping and being late gave me a little more rest and will help me practice using my time efficiently today).

**3.** Teach children strategies to figure out what is causing their negative attitudes, and help them come up with strategies to extinguish the source of the negativity. Though it's not always easy, finding the cause of negativity is much more effective than just focusing on positive thoughts.

**4.** Explain to your child that some causes of a negative attitude are internal as opposed to external. A person who feels unworthy may try to project his/her unworthiness onto a family member or close friend. This can lead to feelings of anger toward that person. If the cause is internal, start by working on yourself first!

**5.** Strongly encourage children to control their inner monologues (i.e., "I'm so bad at math!"). Negative "I" statements can lead directly to a hopeless, negative attitude.

**6.** Remind children they cannot control everything; but they can control how they choose to feel about an event. *"Staying angry at another person is like drinking poison and expecting the other person to suffer." – Author Unknown*

**7.** Create a positive environment (home, school) for children. The negative apple usually doesn't fall far from the tree!

**8.** Provide children with genuine affection, kind words, hugs, love and positive nurturing.

**9.** Help children develop hobbies and skills that can increase their confidence. It's easier to have a positive attitude when you feel accomplished.

**10.** Point out attitude displayed by other people (both positive and negative). Remember… *"There are some people who are on this planet to show the rest of us how NOT to be!" – Julia Cook*

For more parenting information, visit boystown.org/parenting.

*"Life is 10% what happens to me and 90% how I react to it!"* – Charles Swindoll

# Boys Town Press Books by Julia Cook
## Kid-friendly books to teach social skills

*A book series to help kids take responsibility for their behavior.*

  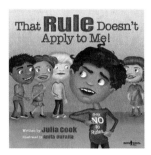  

978-1-934490-80-8    978-1-934490-90-7    978-1-934490-98-3    978-1-944882-08-2    978-1-944882-09-9

  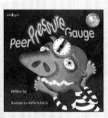   

**Building** RELATIONSHIPS

*A book series to help kids get along.*

Other Titles:
Cliques Just Don't Make Cents and Hygene You Stink!

978-1-934490-30-3    978-1-934490-47-1    978-1-934490-48-8    978-1-934490-86-0    978-1-934490-97-6    978-1-944882-05-1

To reinforce the social skills RJ learns in each book, accompanying poster sets and activity guides are available.

COMMUNICATE *with* **Confidence**

*A book series to help kids master the art of communicating*

978-1-934490-20-4    978-1-934490-43-3    978-1-934490-49-5    978-1-934490-67-9    978-1-934490-57-0    978-1-934490-76-1    978-1-934490-58-7

*Other Titles:* I Just Don't Like the Sound of NO!, Sorry, I Forgot to Ask!, and Teamwork Isn't My Thing, and I Don't Like to Share!

31901060905298

BoysTownPress.org

**For information on Boys Town, its Education Model®, Common Sense Parenting®, and training programs:**
boystowntraining.org | boystown.org/parenting
training@BoysTown.org | 1-800-545-5771

**For parenting and educational books and other resources:**
BoysTownPress.org
btpress@BoysTown.org | 1-800-282-6657